There is always room at our table for the hungry and lonely.
For the Brantleys, Busbys, Barclays, Currys, Freemans,
Hungs, Jeans, Johnsons, Millers, Newtons,
Portifields, Skaras, and Thornhills.
Sunday dinner would not be the same without you.
Special thanks to Coy and Lori
—V.B.N.

Don't Let Auntie Mabel Bless the Table

Bless the Table

Vanessa Brantley Newton

🍎 Blue Apple Books

Sunday dinner is always a treat.
We go to Auntie Mabel's. We're ready to eat.

Everyone is seated at the table—
everyone except dear Auntie Mabel.

She is bringing mashed potatoes,
And a bowl of stewed tomatoes.

Poppa says,
"It's time to pray.

Let's give thanks for this good day."

We all bow our heads in prayer—
Auntie Mabel's voice fills the air.

"God is great. God is good.
We thank him for this food.
By his hand must all be fed.
Give us, Lord, our daily bread."

"Now bless the corn and black-eyed peas,
Virginia ham, and mac and cheese.

Bless the roast chicken—
it's much too small.
I'm sure, Lord,
it won't feed us all."

"Bless the yams,
sweet and sticky.
Bless the Brussels sprouts,
so, so icky.

Bless the carrots
and collard greens.
Bless the gravy
and lima beans.

Bless the beets
and pickled pigs' feet.
Bless the meal
we are about to eat."

"Dear LORD,

Bless the children
and grown-ups, too.
Remember little Bobby
in Timbuktu.
Bless the President
of the United States.
Mama thinks he has
a kind face.

Bless the schools
and all the teachers.
Bless Pastor Bob—
he's a swell preacher!
Bless everyone sitting
at this table.
And please
don't forget me . . .

AUNTIE MABEL!"

"Lord, bless the chairs, and bless the . . . "

Poppa stands up
and clears his throat.
"To Auntie Mabel,
I'd like to say,
Gracing the table
shouldn't take all day!"

"The food is cold.
We'll have to reheat it,

before anyone here
can begin to eat it."

"Sorry," says Auntie Mabel.
"I didn't mean to pray so long.
I really intended to sing a song."

"Please, Mabel.
DON'T SING!"

"Let's pray,"
says Poppa.

"Bless everyone
at our table.
And, Lord, don't forget
Auntie Mabel."

AMEN!

First Edition
Printed in China 09/10
ISBN: 978-1-60905-029-0

1 3 5 7 9 10 8 6 4 2

E 19

Distributed in the U.S. by Chronicle Books